For Claire,
I hope you enjoy learning about
Theodoric and rainbows. Happy reading!
            Best wishes,
            Stephen Kramer
            11-16-95

*written by*

**Stephen Kramer**

*illustrated by*

**Daniel Mark Duffy**

# Theodoric's
# Rainbow

W. H. FREEMAN AND COMPANY  ◆  NEW YORK

Seven hundred years ago, the cities of Europe were surrounded by walls. Kings and emperors ruled the land. Knights rode their horses through the countryside. And a man named Theodoric of Freiberg lived and studied in Germany.

Theodoric was a Dominican friar. Like other friars, he spent much of his life in worship. When the chapel bell rang, Theodoric walked to church with the other friars.

Theodoric sang in the choir. He taught the young friars and preached in village churches on Sundays. He prayed whenever he could.

But Theodoric also set aside time to read and study.

Theodoric was a curious man. When he looked up at the sun and clouds, he saw a sky full of questions. Why does the sun sometimes have a halo? he wondered. Why are there colors around the stars on misty nights? How does light travel through the air?

Of all the shapes and colors he saw overhead, Theodoric was most curious about rainbows. To him, the bows of light that appeared among the clouds were the most beautiful sight in the sky.

People told many different stories about rainbows. For Brother John, a rainbow was a glimpse of heaven.

"Look," he said whenever a rainbow appeared. "God has opened a door in the sky, and light from heaven is shining down on Earth."

"In the village where I grew up," said Brother Jacob, "farmers say the rainbow is a serpent that lives in the sky and drinks water from the rivers and lakes."

"My grandmother told me that fairies put rainbows in the sky," said Brother Gregory. "She said that where a rainbow has touched the ground you can find a handful of pearls."

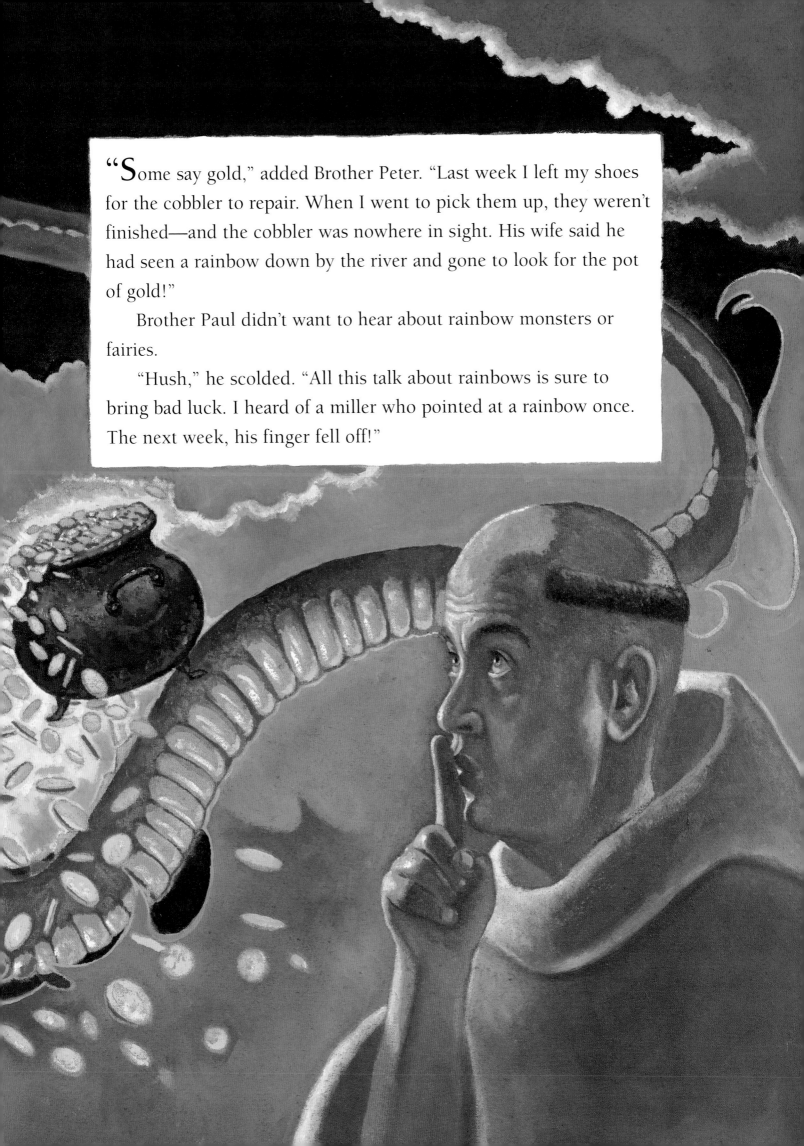

"Some say gold," added Brother Peter. "Last week I left my shoes for the cobbler to repair. When I went to pick them up, they weren't finished—and the cobbler was nowhere in sight. His wife said he had seen a rainbow down by the river and gone to look for the pot of gold!"

Brother Paul didn't want to hear about rainbow monsters or fairies.

"Hush," he scolded. "All this talk about rainbows is sure to bring bad luck. I heard of a miller who pointed at a rainbow once. The next week, his finger fell off!"

Theodoric didn't believe the stories about rainbows. Tales about magical snakes and fairy treasure were fun to hear, but Theodoric wanted to know how and why the beautiful bands of colored light appeared in the sky.

So Theodoric read what the ancient Greeks had written about rainbows. He read what Arab scholars had written about the light and colors that rainbows are made of. And he studied the writings of others who had tried to understand rainbows.

But Theodoric didn't find the answers to his rainbow questions in any of the books he read. If I want to learn about rainbows, Theodoric finally decided, I'm going to have to study them myself.

Brother Paul was nervous when he heard the news. "Study rainbows?" he exclaimed. "Not here, I hope!"

Brother Gregory laughed. "Just keep your hands in your pockets," he said to Brother Paul. "I'm sure your fingers will be safe."

"But tell me, Brother Theodoric," asked Brother John, "how can you study a rainbow? It is too far away to hold or touch. Do you have a ladder that reaches to heaven?"

"I don't need a ladder to heaven," replied Theodoric. "There are rainbows right here on the ground."

"Every morning, when sunlight shines on the dewdrops, there are rainbow colors in the grass. There are rainbow colors in a spider's web. There are rainbow colors in the spray from the mill wheel.

"I can see rainbows and colors when sunlight shines on drops of water," Theodoric said, "so I will learn about rainbows by studying what happens to light when it shines on a single drop of water."

Every afternoon, when the sun was low enough to shine into his room, Theodoric went to work. He hung heavy, dark curtains over his window, folding back one corner just enough for a beam of sunlight to enter the darkness. Next, he filled a round glass container with water and placed it in the path of the sunlight.

Theodoric moved this giant raindrop back and forth. He shined light on the drop from above. He shined light on the drop from below. He watched where the light entered the raindrop. And he watched where the light shined back out.

Sometimes the other friars looked up at Theodoric's window.

"What is Brother Theodoric doing?" asked Brother Frederick.

"Maybe he likes to pray in the dark," said Brother Peter.

"Maybe he's resting," said Brother Charles.

"Brother Theodoric is not resting," said Brother Paul, "and he's not praying. Brother Theodoric is making a rainbow in his room!"

As Theodoric worked, he made drawings. Soon he had tablets filled with pictures of giant raindrops. Theodoric saw that sunlight bent a little when it entered a raindrop near the top. And he saw that the drop could make rainbow colors when sunlight shined on it in a certain way. But he still couldn't figure out how a rainbow appeared in the sky.

Theodoric began to think about light and raindrops more and more. He thought about rainbows when he ate, when he taught, and when he walked in the country. Theodoric went to bed thinking about rainbows, and he woke up thinking about rainbows.

One afternoon, Theodoric sat in the darkness experimenting with his raindrop. As he moved the raindrop back and forth in the sunlight, he watched the rainbow colors that appeared on his robe. Suddenly, Theodoric stopped. He stared at the raindrop for a moment.

"The light bounces off the back," he said to himself. "The light comes into the raindrop near the top, bounces off the back, and comes out near the bottom!" Theodoric kneeled beside the table, carefully putting his face into the exact spot where the rainbow colors had shined onto his robe. Closing one eye, Theodoric stared into the raindrop.

A shiver of excitement ran through Theodoric's body. "There's the red," he whispered. "When my eye is here, I see only red light reflected from the raindrop."

He moved his head up just a bit. "Now it's yellow," he said out loud. "From here, I can see only the yellow light."

Theodoric moved his head twice more. "Green," he said, "and blue." He sat back on his heels in amazement.

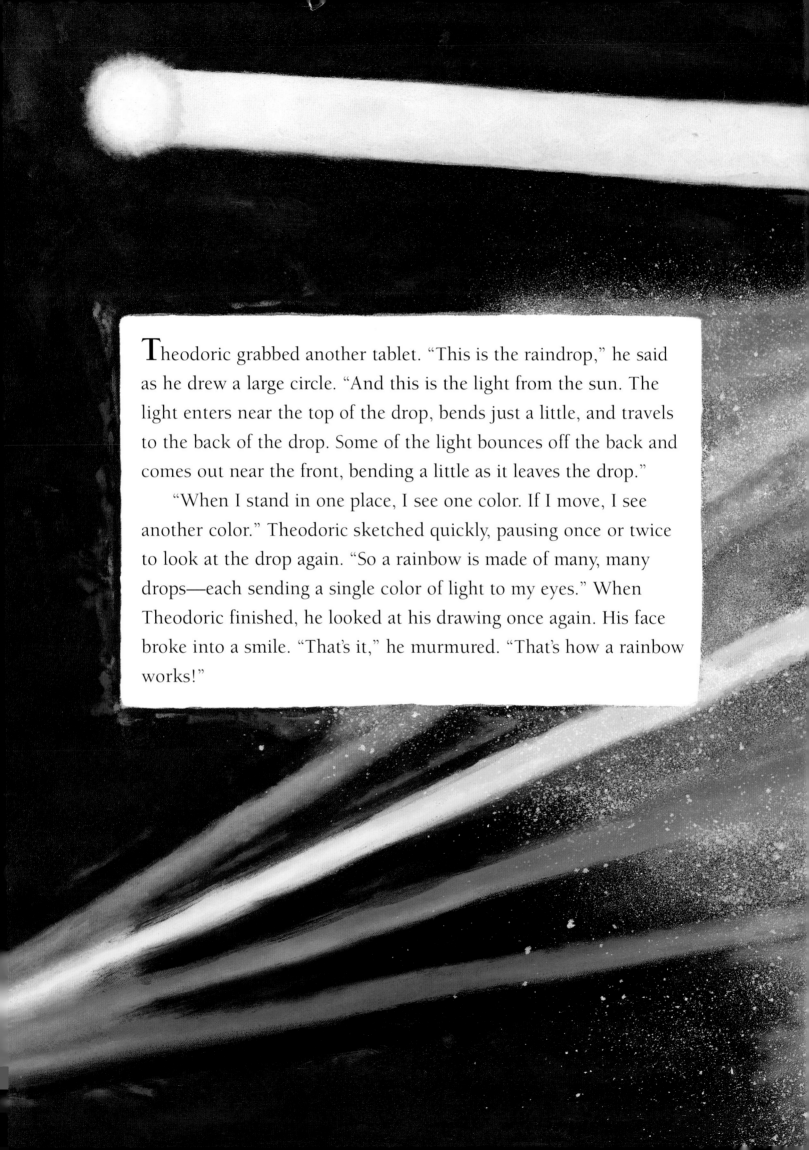

Theodoric grabbed another tablet. "This is the raindrop," he said as he drew a large circle. "And this is the light from the sun. The light enters near the top of the drop, bends just a little, and travels to the back of the drop. Some of the light bounces off the back and comes out near the front, bending a little as it leaves the drop."

"When I stand in one place, I see one color. If I move, I see another color." Theodoric sketched quickly, pausing once or twice to look at the drop again. "So a rainbow is made of many, many drops—each sending a single color of light to my eyes." When Theodoric finished, he looked at his drawing once again. His face broke into a smile. "That's it," he murmured. "That's how a rainbow works!"

"**B**rothers!" said Theodoric. "I have something to show you."

"What is it?" asked Brother John.

"Come with me," said Theodoric.

"You've discovered how rainbows form?" asked Brother John, hurrying after him.

"I guess Brother Theodoric hasn't been resting," said Brother Charles.

"Or praying," said Brother Peter.

"Oh, dear," said Brother Paul, staying a safe distance behind. "Oh, dear!"

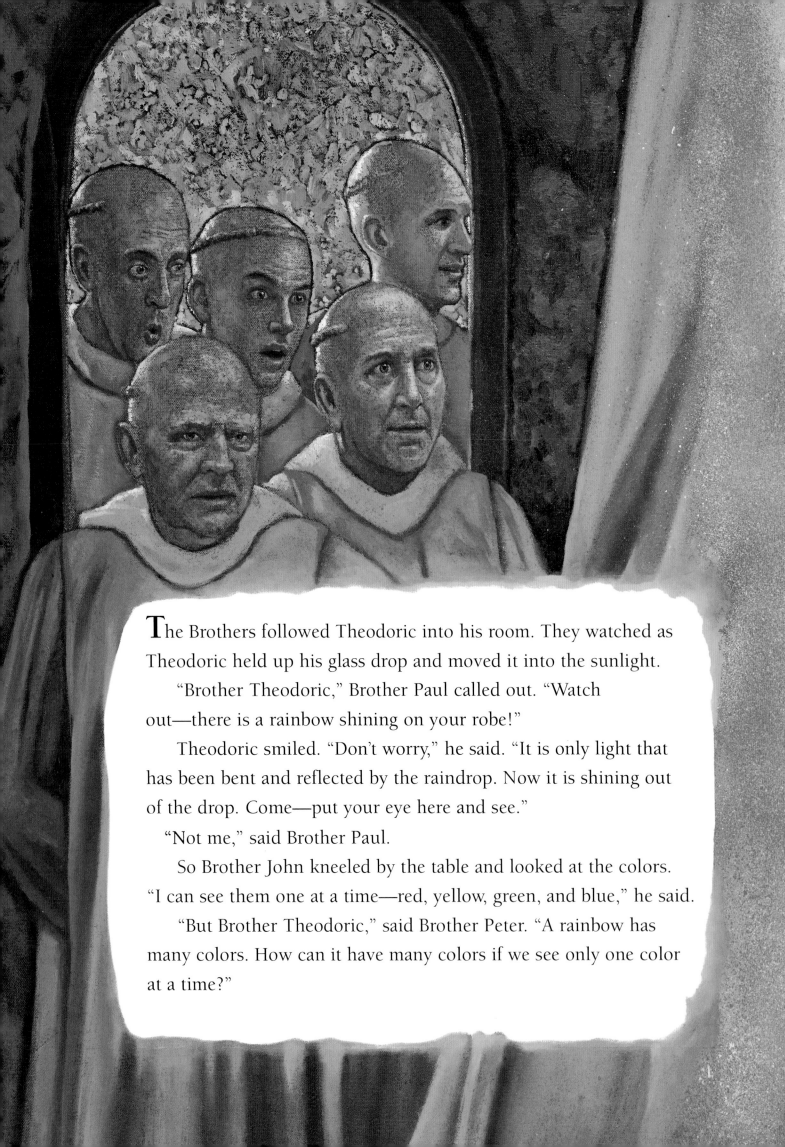

The Brothers followed Theodoric into his room. They watched as Theodoric held up his glass drop and moved it into the sunlight.

"Brother Theodoric," Brother Paul called out. "Watch out—there is a rainbow shining on your robe!"

Theodoric smiled. "Don't worry," he said. "It is only light that has been bent and reflected by the raindrop. Now it is shining out of the drop. Come—put your eye here and see."

"Not me," said Brother Paul.

So Brother John kneeled by the table and looked at the colors. "I can see them one at a time—red, yellow, green, and blue," he said.

"But Brother Theodoric," said Brother Peter. "A rainbow has many colors. How can it have many colors if we see only one color at a time?"

Theodoric showed the Brothers his drawings. "See," he said, "each drop of water reflects all the rainbow colors. But from any one place, you can see only one color from each drop. The light from drops in different parts of the sky makes up the bands of the rainbow."

"Look," said Brother John, cupping his hands around the colored light. "Brother Theodoric has captured a rainbow. He has brought heaven's light right into this room!"

Brother Paul shook his head. "I never dreamed I'd see such a thing," he said. "You hold the rainbow if you like, Brother John. I'm not going one step closer."

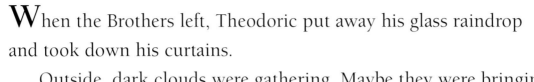

When the Brothers left, Theodoric put away his glass raindrop and took down his curtains.

Outside, dark clouds were gathering. Maybe they were bringing rain. And maybe the rain would fall while the sun was still shining.

Theodoric reached for his tunic. It was the kind of sky in which a rainbow might appear. And if a rainbow appeared, Theodoric was going to be there to see it.

## About Theodoric of Freiburg

Theodoric (also known as Dietrich) of Freiburg was a German philosopher and theologian who lived from about 1250 A.D. to about 1311 A.D. Although Theodoric is the author of more than thirty works on metaphysics and optics, little is known of his personal life.

*De Iride et Radialibus Impressionibus*, Theodoric's book about rainbows, was written shortly after 1304 A.D. While most other scholars were still using philosophy and discussion to try to understand natural phenomena, Theodoric was studying rainbows by doing experiments with light, crystals, and glass globes filled with water. Theodoric's discoveries about how light is reflected and refracted by drops of water gave him the information he needed to propose the first geometrically correct explanation of the rainbow.

No one knows, any more, exactly where or how Theodoric made his discoveries. No one knows whom he shared his discoveries with, or how some of his superstitious friends may have reacted. This is the story of how it might have happened.

*To Chris, with love—S.K.*

*To John and Luke, and that lady on the hill,*
*for always being there. —D. M. D.*

With thanks to Father Hugh Feiss, Librarian, Mt. Angel Abbey, and Barbara Hurwitz Grant, Cornell University, for their help with this book.

Text copyright © 1995 by Stephen Kramer. Art copyright © 1995 by Daniel Mark Duffy. All rights reserved.

**Scientific American Books for Young Readers** is an imprint of
W. H. Freeman and Company, 41 Madison Avenue, New York, NY 10010.

Art direction by Maria Epes. Book design by Debora S. Smith.

**Library of Congress Cataloging-in-Publication Data**

Kramer, Stephen P.

Theodoric's rainbow / written by Stephen Kramer ; illustrated by Daniel Mark Duffy.

Summary: Theodoric of Freiberg, a Dominican friar of the early fourteenth century, discovers how sunlight and drops of water make rainbows.

ISBN 0-7167-6603-5 (hc)

1. Dietrich, von Freiberg, ca. 1250-ca. 1310—Juvenile fiction. [1. Theodoric of Freiberg, ca. 1250-ca. 1310—Fiction. 2. Rainbow—Fiction. 3. Friars—Fiction.] I. Duffy, Daniel M., ill. II. Title.

PZ7.K85893th  1995                                                                                                95-11469
[Fic]—dc20                                                                                                               CIP
                                                                                                                              AC

Printed in the United States of America.
10  9  8  7  6  5  4  3  2  1